HOP
ON
POP

By Dr. Seuss

I CAN READ IT ALL BY MYSELF

Beginner Books

This edition produced for The Book People Ltd,
Hall Wood Avenue, Haydock, St Helens WA11 9UL

Trademark Random House Inc.
Authorised user HarperCollins*Publishers* Ltd

4 6 8 10 9 7 5 3

ISBN 0 583 32421 5

© 1963, 1991 by Dr. Seuss Enterprises, L.P.
All Rights Reserved
A Beginner Book published by arrangement with
Random House Inc., New York, USA
First published in the UK 1964

Printed and bound in Hong Kong

UP
PUP

Pup is up.

CUP
PUP

Pup in cup

PUP
CUP

Cup on pup

MOUSE
HOUSE

Mouse on house

HOUSE
MOUSE

House on mouse

ALL
TALL

We all are tall.

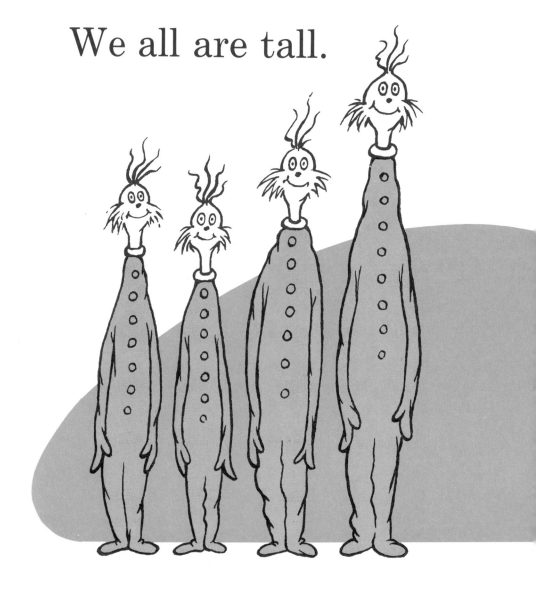

ALL
SMALL

We all are small.

ALL
BALL

We all play ball

BALL
WALL

up on a wall.

12

ALL
FALL

Fall off the wall

DAY
PLAY

We play all day.

NIGHT
FIGHT

We fight all night.

HE
ME

He is after me.

HIM
JIM

Jim is after him.

SEE
BEE

We see a bee.

SEE
BEE
THREE

Now we
see three.

THREE
TREE

Three fish in a tree

Fish in a tree?
How can that be?

RED
RED

They call me Red.

RED
BED

I am in bed.

RED
NED
TED
and
ED
in
BED

24

PAT
PAT

They call him Pat.

PAT
SAT

Pat sat on hat.

PAT
CAT

Pat sat on cat.

PAT
BAT

Pat sat on bat.

NO
PAT
NO

Don't sit on that.

31

SAD

DAD

BAD

HAD

Dad is sad
very, very sad.
He had a bad day.
What a day Dad had!

THING
THING

What is that thing?

THING
SING

That thing can sing!

SONG
LONG

A long, long song

Good-by, Thing.
You sing too long.

WALK
WALK

We like to walk.

WALK
TALK

We like to talk.

HOP
POP

We like to hop.
We like to hop
on top of Pop.

STOP

You must not
hop on Pop.

Mr. BROWN
Mrs. BROWN

Mr. Brown upside down

Pup up

Brown down

Pup is down.
Where is Brown?

45

WHERE IS BROWN?
THERE IS BROWN!

Mr. Brown is out of town.

BACK
BLACK

Brown came back.

Brown came back
with Mr. Black.

SNACK SNACK

Eat a snack.

Eat a snack
with Brown and Black.

JUMP
BUMP

He jumped.
He bumped.

FAST
PAST

He went past fast.

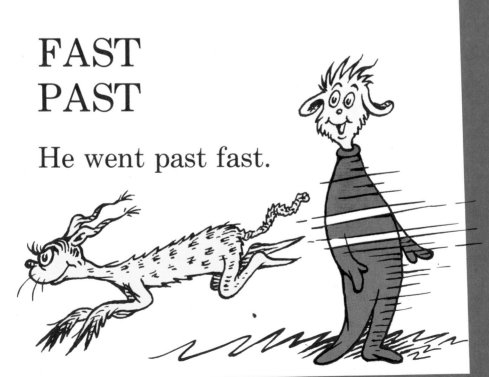

WENT
TENT
SENT

He went into the tent.

I sent him out of the tent.

WET
GET

Two dogs get wet.

HELP
YELP

They yelp for help.

HILL
WILL

Will went up the hill.

WILL
HILL
STILL

Will is
up the hill still.

FATHER
MOTHER

SISTER
BROTHER

That one is
my other brother.

My brothers read
a little bit.

Little
words
like

If and it.

My father
can read
big words, too

like......••••••••

CONSTANTINOPLE

and

TIMBUKTU

SAY
SAY

What does this say?

seehemewe
patpuppop
hethreetreebee
tophopstop

Ask me tomorrow
but not today.

64